the story of chess

Horacio Cardo
the story of chess

Abbeville Press Publishers
New York London Paris

8

This is the story of the game of chess, or at least the story as it was told to me when I was a child. They say it began a long time ago, before there were books or even the written word. It is the story of two nations, one black and the other white, that lived on and fought over a great island that has since disappeared.

They say that so many people died in the war and that the sadness of the two kings was so great that they decided to leave a tribute to the war so that it would not be repeated. The kings knew the task would not be an easy one, so they offered a large reward to the person who could tell the story in an original and memorable way.

From that moment on, inventors, jesters, and storytellers began to parade before the court, but none of them could devise a fitting memorial. So much time passed that the kings were losing hope of ever seeing their wishes fulfilled.

Then one day a man named Sissa came into the kingdom and declared that he had the answer to all the royal wishes. When the two courts, bored and skeptical as they had become, were brought together the stranger spoke: "The story you request is locked inside this wooden case." He then placed a box and a playing board at the feet of the kings.

the board

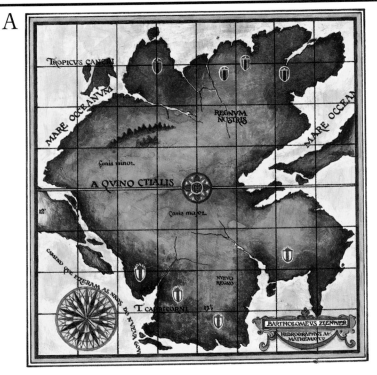

"The board," he explained, "is a replica of this island, divided by seven parallels and seven meridians, just like a map, and makes equal numbers of light and dark squares, sixty-four in all. The squares are placed in an alternating pattern in such a way that the white square is at the near right of each of the two players."

"The events are told in the form of a game. The playing pieces are simple wood figurines," Sissa added, turning the box upside down in a shower of pieces that represented every one of the members of the court. "They will relive the battle every time the game is played, making their moves just as they did in real life."

With the back of his hand he then swept away all of the pieces and set only one of them back on the board.

"To play this game," he said, "we must learn the moves of each and every one of your pieces. Are you ready?"

With great excitement, all present agreed and sat down around the storyteller.

C

II

the King

Placing his index finger on the crown of the figure resting on the board, the newcomer continued his tale: "This is one of the kings of this story. There are two, one for each side: one black and the other white. They move in identical fashion and are the most important figures in the game. As such, I have given them all of the strategic moves. Befitting the cautious exercise of a king's judgment, they will be able to move a distance of one square with every turn." The vanity of the kings was seen to be immediately placated.

"But despite all his royal majesty," Sissa continued, "the King cannot play alone. He needs, at the very least, the presence of his counterpart on the field of battle. That is to say, the other King."

After brief reflection, he proceeded: "The animosity of these kings has run so deep that they have been condemned to remain apart forever, separated by at least one square. On the game board they will never be able to occupy adjacent squares."

"That seems just to me," said one of the kings.

"To me, too," said the other.

"It is just," the storyteller responded. "But in order to carry out the most elementary of battles, they will require the assistance of one of the members of their court."

After studying the situation carefully, the advisors to both kings reached the same conclusion. The narrator paused, withdrew the kings from the board, and replaced them with two new pieces.

the Queen

"These are the queens," he said. "Like the kings, there are also two: one for each color. They are the most powerful figures in their respective courts. The Queen sparkles and shines like a star; her light permits her to move rapidly in all directions, reaching even the farthest points on the board in a single move."

When confronted with the extraordinary powers assigned to their queens, the consternation of the kings made them fidget nervously on their thrones.

"But we must remember," Sissa said thoughtfully, "that the Queen also is restricted: unlike the King, her presence is not essential to the game."

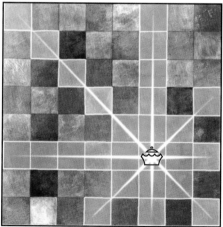

The atmosphere quickly became less tense, and the storyteller then proceeded to remove the Queen from the board.

the bishop

"Each member of the royalty," he continued, "has its own counselor: the Bishop."

He placed a Bishop on the board. Astonished, those in attendance followed with great attention the appearances and disappearances of those little wooden beings coming magically in and out of the box.

"These counselors and messengers, two for each side, four in all, begin the game at the side of their kings and queens in order to whisper advice in their ears. They will move in the direction of their voices. In other words, diagonally. And they can move a great distance, because great is the power of the spoken word."

This move was approved without consultation, because there were no advisers who could decide justly. Then Sissa withdrew the Bishop and continued his story.

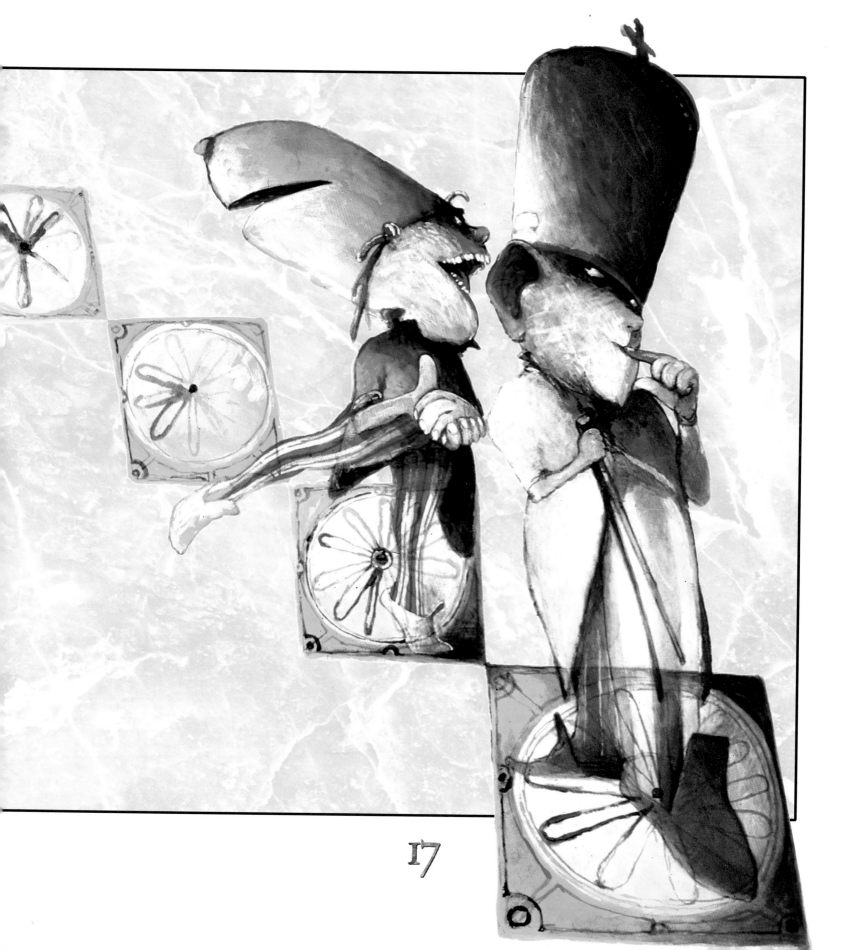

17

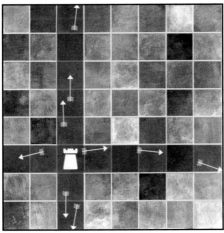

the ROOK

"The combatants situated atop the rooks wield enormous power. They control the points of the compass from their vantage point and can attack the enemy from a great distance."

He then set one of the rooks in the center of the board, saying: "They will move in the pattern of a cross: to the north, to the south, to the east and to the west, and as far as they can see. In other words, to the very edges of the board, as long as another figure doesn't get in their way."

Everyone looked at each other in agreement. It seemed logical.

the knight

The knights were the only ones who held their silence, clearly uncomfortable.

"What's wrong with you," asked one of the kings. "Don't you think the rules of the game are fair?"

"It's not that," they answered. "The only objectionable thing, in our judgment, is that it hasn't left us any move that matches our importance."

"That's not so," the storyteller said. "You are represented in this game by a horse, which is the only piece that jumps."

"Only that? Our power is indeed very great."

"Not as great as your vanity," someone shot back in a loud voice from the back of the room.

A noisy argument ensued. Things didn't seem to be taking a friendly turn, and if an immediate truce wasn't reached, it would all end very badly.

"There's nothing better," the game's inventor said, "than to put this to a test."

"That's it," said the knights. "Let's have a duel between warriors and the one who survives will decide it."

"No more fighting. There will be no more deaths in our kingdoms," the kings declared.

"I don't suggest a fight," Sissa pointed out. "I only propose a test of skill. I invite the knights to choose the best one among them."

After that was done, everybody went to one of the jousting grounds where the challenge would be taken up.

One hour later, spectators who had gathered on top of a wall that surrounded the arena watched as the chosen knight appeared, mounted on a splendid steed. Then came Sissa, bearing a fox in a cage. Once he reached the center of the jousting ground, he released the animal.

"Very well," he exclaimed to the knight. "Your challenge will be to hunt him down."

The knight drew his mount up close in front of the King.

"I have never been so insulted, Your Majesty," he said angrily. "I was not proclaimed a knight in armor in order to challenge a fox."

"We all know of your bravery," the sovereign responded. "But now, do as our guest asks of you."

Somewhat hurt and angry, the knight called on his full dexterity and corralled the fox in one of the corners in a matter of seconds, poised to deliver the fatal blow. The animal, seeing itself lost, scurried under the legs of the horse. Fearing that the fox would injure his stallion, the knight began turning his mount in circles, trying to gain enough distance to use his weapon. And so it went for a long time, the knight always trying to separate himself from the fox while the animal kept itself hidden beneath the horse. Seeing the contest at a stalemate, Sissa told the King: "I believe that will be enough, Your Majesty."

The King could do nothing more than nod agreement.

"Let's return to our game then," the visitor said, turning back toward the palace.

Once there, he continued: "We have all seen clearly the real power of a mounted combatant. He is strong in the fight at middle distance, but he lacks the reach to strike beyond an arm's length. We can also see his clumsiness in fighting at close range.

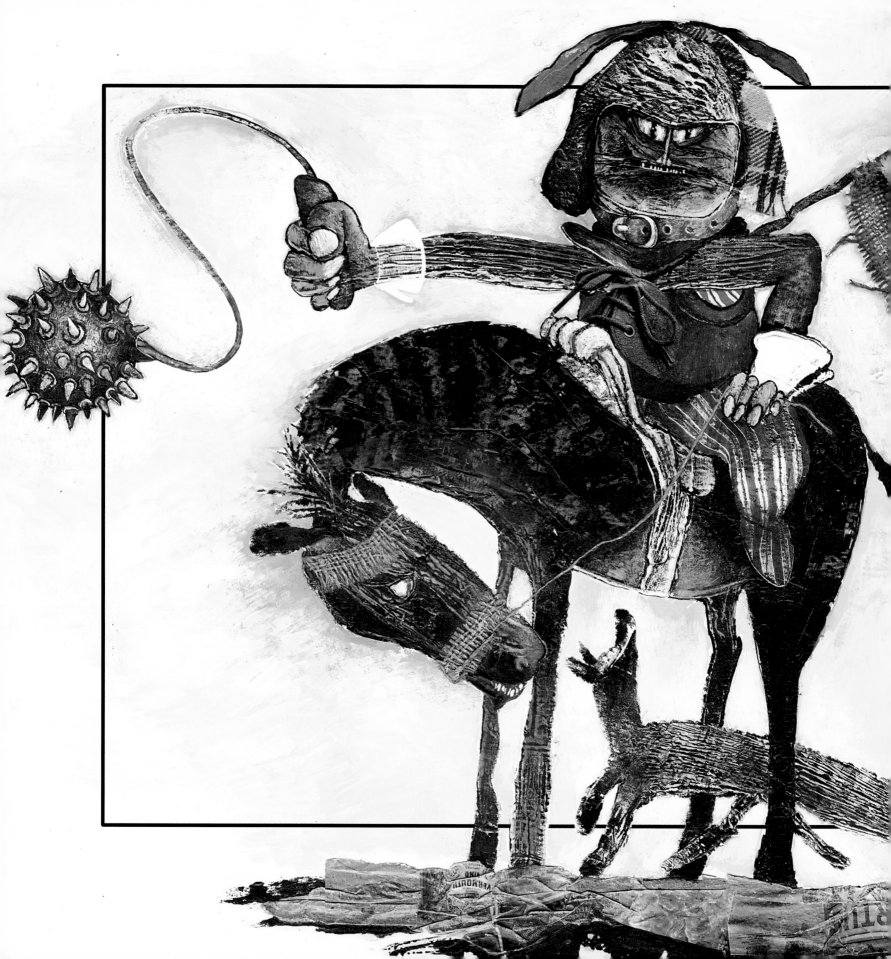

"I think it would be wise therefore to give him a move in which he can jump inside a circle proscribed by the range of his weapon, from a square of one color to a square of the opposite color."

23

Everyone hung on to the words of the storyteller trying to memorize this new and highly specialized move. They thought so long about what he had said that night soon fell and they decided to suspend the demonstration until the following day. Reunited with the courts the next morning, Sissa picked up the thread of his narrative.

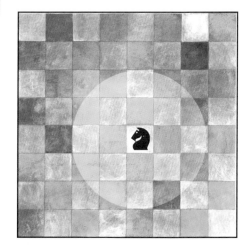

the pawn

"These smallest sixteen figures, eight of each color, are the pawns. They are the foot soldiers, the most numerous force on the board. They move slowly, one square at a time, because they move on foot. And they always proceed straight ahead, loyal to their King, never choosing to turn back."

"It seems that they would suffer the most casualties," one of the kings mused out loud, impressed by the valor of the infantry.

"Generally, they do," the stranger confirmed.

A silence fell over the room.

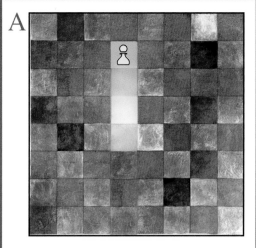

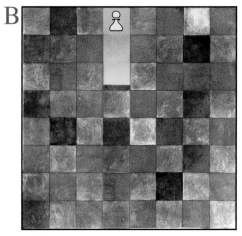

"There should be some way to reward such courage," one of the kings proposed.

"There is. Any pawn that reaches the last enemy defense through successive steps will be instantly converted into any other piece of higher value—with the exception, of course, of the King. Let us call this transformation the coronation of a pawn. And, as we see, it is similar to the King ordaining a knight."

"What do you think of this?" the kings asked the numerous foot soldiers seated to one side of the room.

"For us, it will be an additional honor," they responded without hesitation, "to serve our King as infantry and later to be given a different role."

"Very well then," said the kings.

Seeing how everyone was standing up, the foreigner raised his hand, calling for attention: "I am not done yet," he declared. "It seems you have forgotten the purpose of the game: the war."

Everyone nodded in sober agreement. Sissa continued, "I will now show you certain rules and moves that make up the game. Every piece will attack and defend itself against its rivals according to their respective powers. In other words, when its turn comes up, a figure that encounters a rival in its path will take it prisoner, retire it from the battlefield, and take its place on the board. But this is not obligatory, and each player can decide what to do at every step."

"The pawn, however, will attack diagonally, at a square's distance, because that is how far his weapons reach."

Then he began to set up the figures on the board once again.

"To open the battle," he said, raising the board so everyone could see it, "the pieces must be arranged in the following manner.

"The white King in the black square; the black King in the white square. Because each one will fight to take the domains of his rival.

"The Queens will be positioned beside the Kings, toward the center of the board.

"Arranged at their sides will be the counselors, the Bishops. One will be adviser to the King, the other to the Queen.

"Continuing outward toward either side are the Knights.

"And holding down the corners, the Rooks.

"The Pawns will protect the entire formation from their positions up front.

"After arranging the figures in this pattern," said Sissa, raising his eyes, "the game is played by making their moves in turns, beginning with the white side. The object of the game is to eliminate the enemy King."

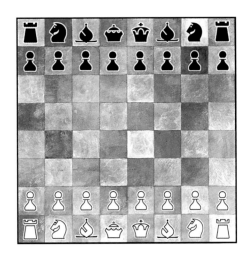

check

"But," somebody interjected, "before you told us that the King could never be captured."

"That's true," the storyteller said. "I said he could never be captured, but he can be checked. Just as the rook does in this case."

Then he showed them the way in which the rook checks the King.

"When he finds himself besieged, the King will be forced to get out of the line of attack immediately, or to shield himself behind one of his lieutenants."

"That doesn't seem to be very regal behavior," somebody called out.

"I don't know what you're talking about," another member of the court answered the heckler. "I believe that any one of us would proudly sacrifice his life for our King."

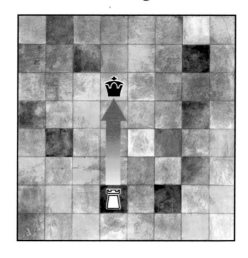

checkmate

The Kings looked all around the room. Those present fell into a hushed silence.

"It seems there is only one person in disagreement," the kings, a little disturbed, told Sissa. "Continue."

"Very well," said the storyteller, resuming with a smile. "When the King can no longer be defended in any way, he is considered fatally wounded and the victory goes to the opposing side. It is called checkmate."

"But war doesn't always end with a victory or a defeat," said somebody who considered himself an expert on the subject. "There are cases, like ours for example, in which no one knows who has triumphed and who has been vanquished."

"The same can occur in this game," the stranger said. "It happens when one of the sides is immobilized in such a way that it can no longer play."

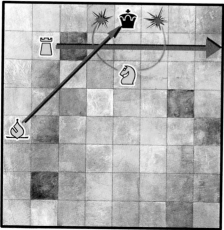

He then gave them the example of two pawns who had blocked and immobilized each other. "If all the pieces on a side find themselves in this situation," he added, "whoever is directing these forces will discover that it is impossible to play any further."

"A draw may also be declared at any point of the game if both players agree that neither of them will be capable of exerting supremacy."

Those listening held their breath, considering all the possibilities of attack and counterattack that this mysterious game presented.

castling

"Our security is fairly precarious in view of these conditions," one of the kings worried out loud.

"In effect, yes," Sissa agreed. "But remember, a King can be attacked or even checked, but never captured. When a King is checked and cannot escape, it is the end of the game."

"Taking all of this into account," he continued, "I have felt it necessary to give the King one more move of additional protection."

"And what is that?" the two kings asked anxiously.

"I have called it castling and it is the only double move in the game. To effect the move, the King must be situated on his original square without having ever moved from it—and with no piece between himself and the rook. This can't be done when the enemy is directly attacking the King or is directly pointed toward any of the squares that the King must cross."

35

"When he thinks his
position is vulnerable," the storyteller continued, "he will do
the following: he will jump
two squares in the direction of
the rook,
which he will then lift,
pass over his head,

and place directly beside
his square toward the center
of the board, blocking all possibility of an attack on that tem-
porary fortress. As we see, it is
very difficult for the King to be
successfully attacked by the
enemy when fortified in such
a way."

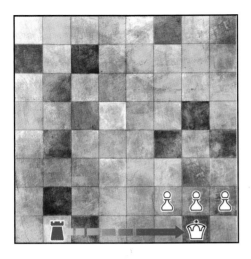

"That's almost magic," exclaimed one of the kings, amazed and pleased.

"And an excellent way of defending oneself," said the other.

"It's both of those things at the same time," Sissa noted. "But one must know when to employ the move and in which direction. If one makes the move at the wrong moment or in the wrong direction, the enemy forces will gather all their strength around the King, and it will be very difficult for him to escape being cornered."

"Once again, you are right," the kings admitted.

The audience continued to murmur about the wonderful possibilities offered by this marvelous game.

But once again, Sissa's voice quieted their comments.

"There are two more exceptional moves that I would like to add, and both belong to the pawns."

"When the pawn is poised to begin, he can choose at the outset whether to move one square in distance or two. These foot soldiers have waited so long and so anxiously to start the battle that when they receive the order to enter into combat, that impetus will make them jump over the first square many times. But this movement is voluntary and each pawn should act in the most suitable manner."

40

in passing

"Many times this headlong rush will make the pawns fall into traps stupidly, and they expose themselves to the attack of rival pawns that have moved beyond the center of the board. A pawn located in any square on its fifth row, seeing an adversary jump and land at his side, can stick out his leg and send the rival piece crashing to the ground. This move is called "in passing," or *en passant*, and it, too, is optional. Many times, these jumps are harmless and one opts to ignore them, choosing instead to use one's move for some greater purpose. Nevertheless, this capture can only be executed in the moment when the adversary makes the leap. After the turn, the possibility vanishes."

A   B   C

"And so," he concluded, "I end by giving the rules of the game, which will be played in a different style by every competitor, in accordance with his personality. Through practice, he will learn to take advantage of his strengths and to overcome his weaknesses."

The Kings, so pleased were they with the cleverness of the game, offered Sissa any compensation that he desired.

"It will be enough for me if you continue to play the game and try to understand its teachings," he responded.

"Is that all you ask?" the Kings exclaimed.

"It is no small task," he answered. "There is no treasure that can compare with the riches within this game."

"What are you saying?" they asked, laughing. "In our two kingdoms there is enough gold to build a palace of the stuff."

"Very well, then," said Sissa, shrugging his shoulders. "May I ask then for a gold coin for every square on this board, added up in geometric progression?"

"If that is all you desire," the Kings answered magnanimously, "so be it."

And they ordered calculations to be made.

The experts began counting immediately: one gold coin for the first square; two for the second; four for the third; sixteen for the fourth—continuously multiplying the previous figure by itself—256 for the fifth; 65,536 for the sixth; 42,949,672 for the seventh, and so on.

After only the first row, the total was already alarming: 261,776,911,311,344. But upon reaching the sixty-fourth, and last, square the figure was so great that it vastly exceeded the sum of all the treasures in all the kingdoms on Earth.

Perhaps because of that, the game is still being played today and will continued to be played as long as man lives.

Editor: Owen Dugan
Production Editor: Meredith Wolf Schizer
Production Manager: Lou Bilka

Computer assistants to Horacio Cardo:
Samanta Cardo, Fernando Lagos, Pablo Ruiz

First edition
2 4 6 8 10 9 7 5 3 1

Library of Congress Cataloging-in-Publication Data
available upon request

ISBN 0-7892-0250-6

44

Cast of Characters

The King

The Rook

The Queen

The Pawn

The Knight

The Bishop

45